PEAS

in a

Pod

For Team TNT. You know why. —TM

To my mother, Elizabeth — there are not enough words but there are always pictures. —TS

First published 2015

EK Books
an imprint of Exisle Publishing Pty Ltd
'Moonrising', Narone Creek Road,
Wollombi, NSW 2325, Australia
P.O. Box 60-490, Titirangi
Auckland 0642, New Zealand
www.ekbooks.com.au

A CiP record for this book is available from the National Library of Australia

ISBN 978 1 921966 71 2

Design and layout by Tina Snerling
Typeset in Daisy's Delights and Duck Tape
Printed in China

This book uses paper sourced under ISO 14001 guidelines from well-managed
forests and other controlled sources.

10 9 8 7 6 5 4 3 2

PEAS in a Pod

Tania McCartney and Tina Snerling

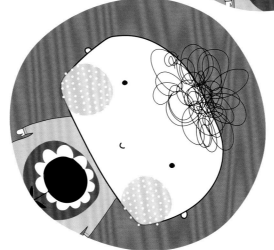

When Pippa, Pia, Poppy, Polly and Peg were born...

... they looked the same.

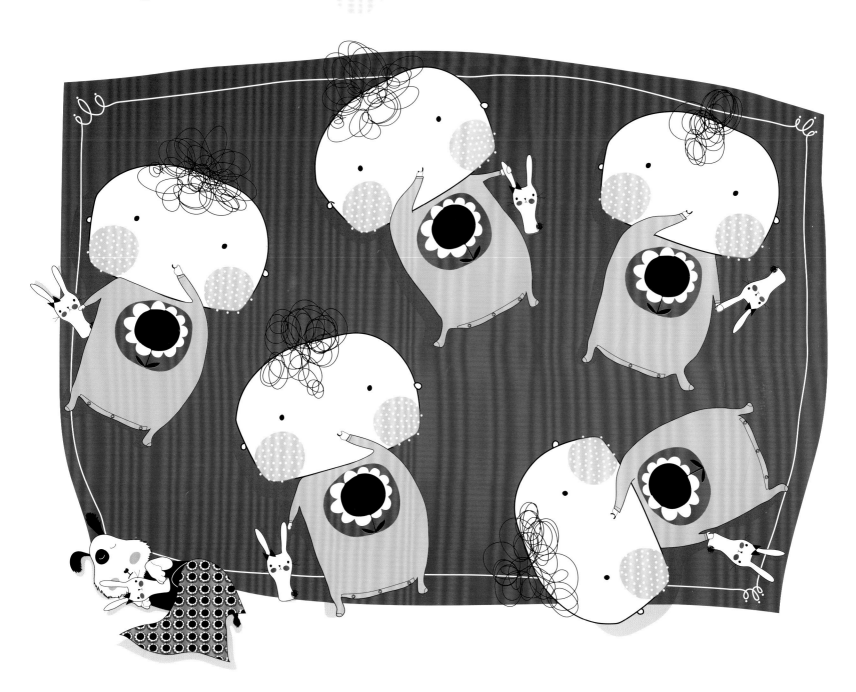

They did everything the same.

Everything.

eating ...

Sleeping ...

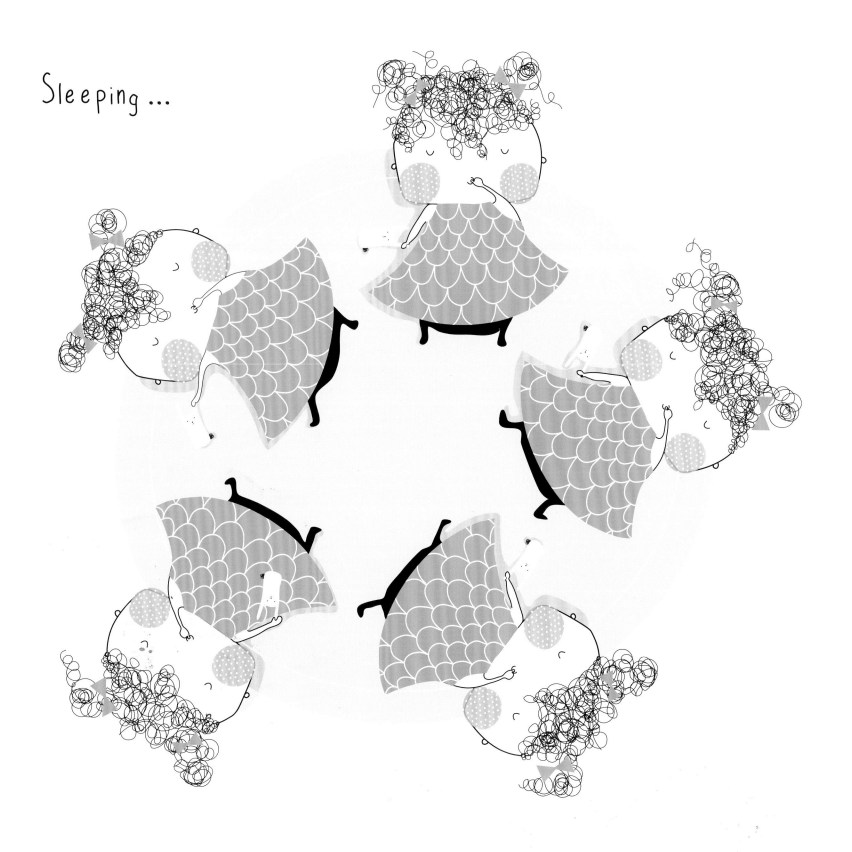

Sitting ...

Then, one fine day, everything changed.

Things became challenging.

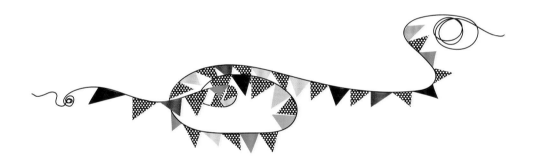

One began overtaking the other.

It was chaos.

So mum and dad stepped in. They put everything right.

And everything became the same again.

Same.

Same.

But Pippa, Pia, Poppy, Polly and Peg didn't like 'same'.

It was time to take control.

First it was the hair.

Then the clothes.

The shoes.

The accessories.

The hobbies.

The activities.

The attitude.

The dreams.

And, more than happily...

Pippa, Pia, Poppy, Polly and Peg were never the same again.

Well, almost ...

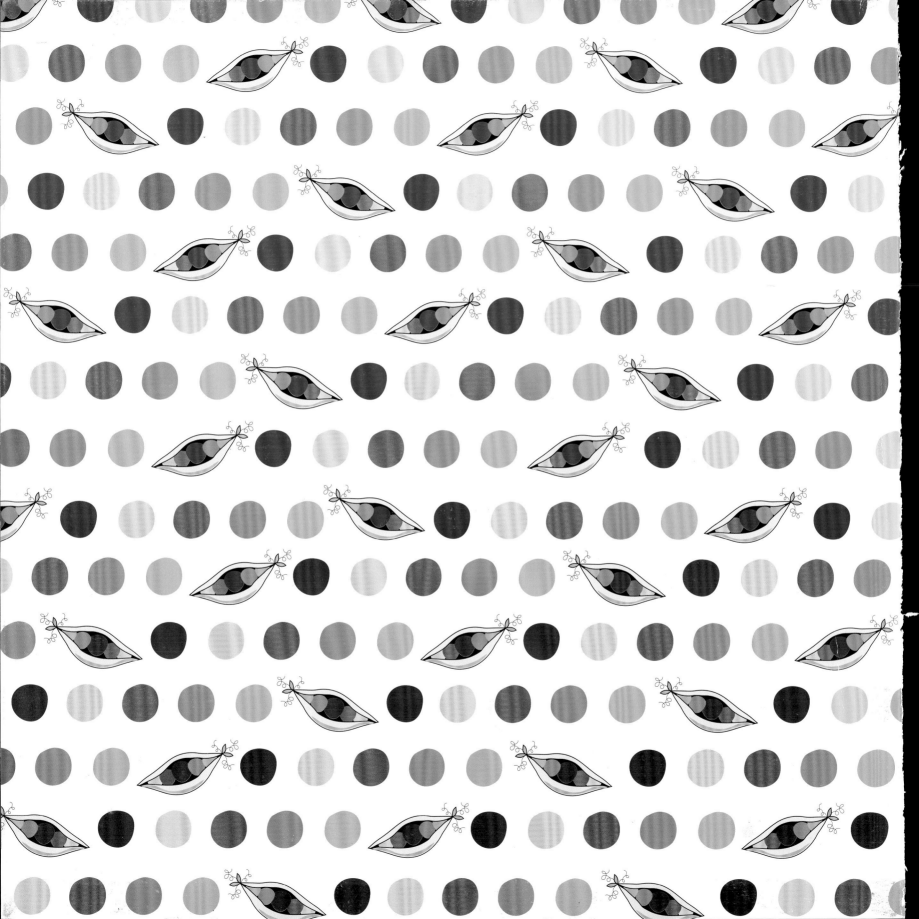